beetle
bop

www.HarcourtBooks.com

Library of Congress Cataloging-in-Publication Data
Fleming, Denise, 1950–
Beetle bop/Denise Fleming.
p. cm.
Summary: Illustrations and rhyming text reveal the great variety
of beetles and their swirling, humming, crashing activities.
[1. Beetles—Fiction. 2. Stories in rhyme.] I. Title.
PZ8.3.F6378Bee 2007
[E]—dc22 2006009756
ISBN 978-0-15-205936-1

A C E G H F D B

Printed in Singapore

The illustrations were created by pouring colored
cotton fiber through hand-cut stencils.

Book design by Denise Fleming and David Powers
Visit www.denisefleming.com.

For David, still the one

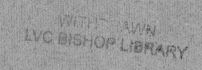

Harcourt, Inc.

Orlando   Austin   New York   San Diego   Toronto   London

DENISE FLEMING

beetle
bop

Striped beetles,

spotted beetles,

all-over-dotted beetles.

Brown beetles,
green beetles,
not-often-seen beetles.

BuZZing beetles,

humming

beetles,

steadily

drumming beetles.

Big beetles,

small **beetles**,

crawl-up-the-wall **beetles.**

chewing beetles,
sawing beetles,

noisily

gnawing

beetles.

Round beetles,
square beetles,
fly-in-the-air beetles.

Bark beetles,

sand beetles,

fill-up-your-hand

beetles.

Diving beetles, whirling beetles,

spiraling, swirling beetles.

Blue beetles,
black beetles,
hide-in-the-crack beetles.

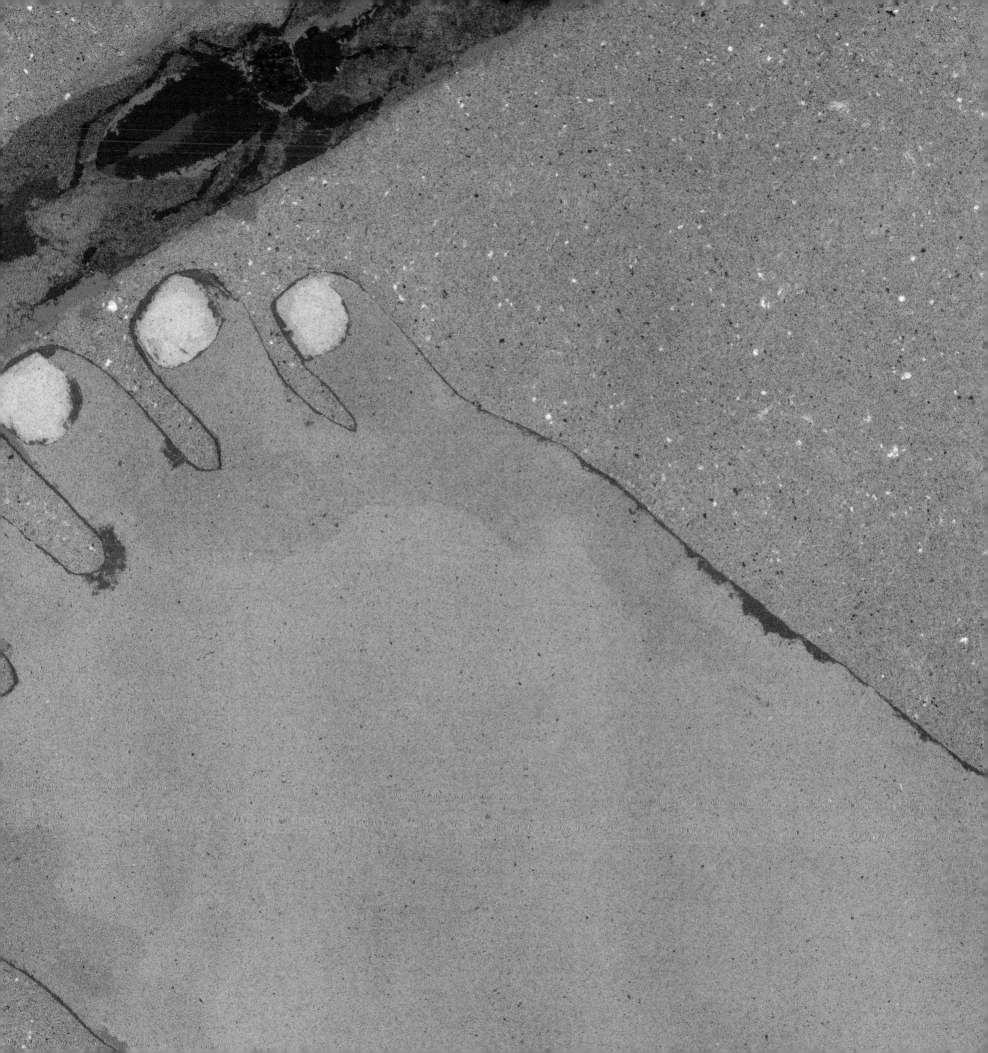

Glowing beetles,
flashing beetles,

constantly crashing
beetles.

Beetles flip.

Beetles flop.

Beetles fly.

Beetles...

Beetles live in forests, deserts, mountains, and ponds. They come in many different shapes, sizes, colors, and patterns. But all beetles have three body segments and six legs, and almost all have two sets of wings—a front set that protects the second set, which is used for flying.

Beetles are one of the largest groups of animals on earth. Some are pests, some are friends.

What kinds of **beetles** live near you?